9/16

Specially Chosen

by

Megan Timm

for the 2016

Summer Reading Program

Super Special #1

Ghost Ship

Ahoy, mateys!

Set sail for a brand-new
adventure with the

PUPPY PIRATES

Coming Soon:

PUPPY 🐾 PIRATES
Super Special #1

Ghost Ship

by Erin Soderberg
illustrations by Russ Cox

A STEPPING STONE BOOK™
Random House 🏠 New York

For Milla, who helped me
create and name the Weirdos.
I love having you as my
writing partner!
—E. S.

Text copyright © 2016 by Erin Soderberg Downing and Robin Wasserman
Cover art copyright © 2016 by Luz Tapia
Interior illustrations copyright © 2016 by Russ Cox

All rights reserved. Published in the United States by Random House
Children's Books, a division of Penguin Random House LLC, New York.

Random House and the colophon are registered trademarks and A Stepping
Stone Book and the colophon are trademarks of Penguin Random House LLC.

Visit us on the Web!
randomhousekids.com
SteppingStonesBooks.com

Educators and librarians, for a variety of teaching tools, visit us at
RHTeachersLibrarians.com

Library of Congress Cataloging-in-Publication Data
Name: Soderberg, Erin.
Title: Ghost ship / Erin Soderberg ; interior illustrations by Russ Cox.
Description: First edition. | New York : Random House, [2016] | Series:
Puppy Pirates super special #1 | Summary: "When Wally is pranked by a
couple of pugs, they accuse him of being more puppy than pirate. How can
Wally prove he's as fearless as the rest? Spending the night on an abandoned
pirate ship should do the trick! But when Wally and his human friend, Henry,
climb aboard, they soon discover the ship might not be so empty after all"
—Provided by publisher.
Indentifiers: LCCN 2015032876 | ISBN 978-1-101-93773-0 (trade) |
ISBN 978-1-101-93774-7 (lib. bdg.) | ISBN 978-1-101-93775-4 (ebook)
Subjects: | JUVENILE FICTION / Action & Adventure / Pirates. | JUVENILE
FICTION / Animals / Dogs. | JUVENILE FICTION / Action & Adventure / General.
Classification: LCC PZ7.S685257 Gh 2016 | DDC [Fic]—dc23

Printed in the United States of America
10 9 8 7 6 5 4 3 2 1
First Edition

This book has been officially leveled by using the F&P Text Level Gradient™
Leveling System.

Random House Children's Books supports the First Amendment and
celebrates the right to read.

CONTENTS

Tail-Tingling Tales

"It was a dark and stormy night ...," Puggly whispered in a spooky voice. "Waves tossed Growlin' Grace's mighty pirate ship to and fro. Thunder *crashed*. Lightning *flashed*!"

Every puppy pirate on board the *Salty Bone* was gathered on the ship's main deck. A fluffy golden retriever named Wally snuggled up to his best mate, a boy named Henry. Big storm clouds filled the afternoon sky. While they waited for the rain to start, the pirates were telling each other scary stories.

Puggly flapped her fancy cape and went on. "Growlin' Grace was the bravest, boldest pirate that ever lived. Lightning didn't scare her. Sea monsters didn't scare her." Thunder rumbled in the distance. Spike the bulldog yelped. Puggly giggled, then said, "Even *thunder* didn't scare Growlin' Grace."

"Thunder doesn't scare me, either," Captain Red Beard barked. The gruff terrier scowled at Puggly. "Isn't this supposed to be a scary story? Stop talking about the weather and get to the spooky part, pug. Ghosties and creepies and such."

"Aye, aye, Captain," Puggly said. "If scary is what you want, scary is what you'll get. Because this is the tale of Growlin' Grace's ghost ship!"

Most of the puppy pirates cheered. But Spike buried his face in his paws. The peg-legged

Bernese mountain dog named Old Salt just yawned. He had lived through so many spooky adventures that nothing scared him anymore.

Puggly sneezed three times before continuing. "Many moons ago, before Old Salt was even born, Growlin' Grace and her crew ruled the seven seas. For many years, they were known as the toughest pirates in all the world. But one dark and stormy night, Growlin' Grace and her crew . . . *disappeared.*"

"We've heard this story!" booed Captain Red Beard. "Tell us a new one."

Puggly shook her head. "You've heard the beginning of this tale, Captain . . . but I bet no one has heard how it ends."

"Tell us!" barked the rest of the pups.

"On that stormy night, Growlin' Grace and her crew set off to find the most fearsome sea creature that ever existed . . . ," Puggly said.

"The Sea Slug!" barked Piggly, Puggly's twin sister.

"That's right." Puggly nodded. "They were searching for the *evil* Sea Slug. Well, when the pups finally tracked down the great and terrible beastie, they were too scared to face it. The Sea Slug was bigger, stronger, and slimier than anything those pirate pups had seen before."

"So what happened?" Wally asked in a whisper. He had never seen the Sea Slug. He hoped he never would.

"Growlin' Grace's crew turned the ship around." Puggly paused. The puppy pirates held their breath, waiting to hear what happened next. "They went against their captain's orders and sailed away. Those pups didn't want to battle the creature because they were afraid."

"Afraid of a slug?" Red Beard barked. "My crew would absotootly never let a slug spook 'em."

"That's what Growlin' Grace thought, too," Puggly continued. "But she was wrong. When the world's greatest pirate captain realized she had a ship full of scaredy-dogs, she kicked 'em all off her ship."

"Because they were scared?" Spike whined. "But the Sea Slug was slimy!"

Puggly nodded. "Yes, sirree. Growlin' Grace didn't like scaredy-dogs. Soon as they found an island, she ordered each and every pup off her ship. Then she set sail alone. Better to have an empty ship, she thought, than a crew of cowards. Her ship sailed on, with Growlin' Grace alone at the wheel."

Wally nuzzled closer against Henry. He thought about how sad it would be to sail the ocean all alone. One of the best things about being a puppy pirate was being part of a crew. The other puppy pirates were his family.

"Now, hundreds of years later, the ghost of Growlin' Grace is still out there somewhere. . . ." The sky had gotten dark while Puggly told her story. Suddenly, a bright flash of lightning ripped through the sky.

Captain Red Beard squirmed under Spike's blanket, whimpering. A gust of wind blasted the deck. Steak-Eye, the ship's cook, spun around

and whipped a wooden spoon through the air like a sword. "En garde!" the tiny Chihuahua growled.

Puggly waited until everything was quiet. Then she whispered, "The ghost of Growlin' Grace still sails the sea, searchin' for worthy pirates. Some night, she might pluck one of *you* out of bed and make you join her ghost crew!"

Piggly howled. "Don't let the ghost of Growlin' Grace get you! *Arrrrrr-ooooo!*"

Giggling Ghost

"Even I have to admit that was a good one, Puggly," Old Salt said gruffly. "Too bad it's not true, eh?"

Not true? Wally let out a happy sigh. It was just a silly, spooky story.

"How do you know it's not true?" Piggly ruffed. "No one knows *for sure* what really happened to Growlin' Grace. Me and Puggly? We think her ghost is still sailing the seven seas."

"Maybe so," Old Salt agreed with a laugh.

Wally told himself that Old Salt was joking. There was no such thing as ghosts.

Thunder boomed, and another flash of lightning lit up the sky. The storm was getting closer. As the other pups scattered to finish their afternoon tasks, Henry and Wally headed down to their bunk for a nap. They had both gotten up early that morning to do their chores.

"Thunderstorms are exciting, don't you think?" Henry said, laying his head on his pillow.

Wally curled up near his best mate and yawned. He was so sleepy, but he wasn't sure he could sleep in a storm. His body shook every time thunder rumbled. He had never liked storms. The loud noises frightened him.

Henry rubbed Wally's fluffy ears and whispered, "In case you were wondering, I love storms. There's nothing to be scared of, mate. Not lightning. Not thunder." Henry flipped over and added, "Gosh, you don't even need to worry about monsters under the bed. I'll keep you safe, mate."

Monsters under the bed? Wally yipped and whimpered. He had never worried about *those* . . . until now!

Wally snuggled close against his friend. His worries kept him awake for a long time. When he finally fell asleep, he tossed and turned. He dreamed of Growlin' Grace and ghost ships, dark skies and rolling waves.

Crrrr-ack!

Thunder and rolling waves pounded at the ship. Wally startled awake, happy to get away from the scary dream he'd been having. In his dream, Growlin' Grace's ghost had come to make him join her crew. Wally tried to settle in and fall asleep again. That's when he heard it. . . .

Ooo-ooh! Woo-ooo! Walllll-ly!

A spooky, ghostly howl filled the room. It was coming from something pale and glowing right next to Wally's bed!

Wally leaped up. His heart was racing. The creature next to the bed was white and spooky. It had an eye patch like Old Salt but seemed to be floating beside the bunk like a ghost. *Growlin' Grace's ghost!* She had come for him!

The ghost pirate swayed and rocked. It howled and moaned. Wally scuttled backward. He got twisted in his blankets and tried to shake loose. Then he yapped to alert Henry to danger. "Ghost pirate!" he barked.

Henry moaned in his sleep, rolled over, and rubbed his eyes. Wally tugged at his friend's sleeve with his teeth. Finally, Henry opened his eyes. He leaped off the bed and faced the ghost pirate. The ghost pirate moaned . . . then giggled.

A giggling ghost? Wally wondered. That's

when he realized just how *small* the ghost pirate was. It didn't even come up to Henry's waist! Wally hopped off the bunk and sniffed at the ghost.

Pug! He smelled pug.

Wally chomped down on the edge of the ghostly white sheet and yanked.

"Piggly?" Wally barked as the ghost costume dropped to the floor. The troublemaking pug was still giggling.

"I got you!" she howled. "You actually thought Growlin' Grace's ghost was comin' to get you? You're not brave enough for her ship. You were scared of a pug playin' dress-up, kid!"

Wally couldn't believe this was just another pug prank! "I *am* brave enough," he growled.

"Is that so?" Piggly laughed. "Why don't you prove it, then?"

"I will," Wally yipped back. "Uh . . . how?"

"I dare you to go down into the belly of the ship—where Steak-Eye keeps his meat. It's pitch-black down there. Scarier than anything. Bilge rats the size of bulldogs!"

Wally knew that couldn't be true. Piggly was just trying to scare him. Probably. He told himself he wasn't afraid of the dark or the giant rats. He would show Piggly just how brave he was. He nudged Henry toward the door. It was easier to be brave when your best friend was with you.

"Bring back a steak to prove you were down there," Piggly said.

With Henry close at his heels, Wally raced down the stairs to the belly of the ship. He and Henry had hidden out in Steak-Eye's storage room when they first stowed away on the *Salty Bone*. The room was warm and snuggly, and it didn't scare him at all. Not usually. But in the storm, it was darker than ever. The shadows flickered. The floorboards creaked and moaned.

Wally padded down, down, down to the bottom of the ship.

Grrrrrrrr.

Wally froze. It sounded like an animal, but what kind? Was that the sound a bilge rat made when it was the size of a bulldog? Could Piggly have been telling the truth? He went down another step. There was a clattering noise in the darkness. Then a rattle. Then . . .

Grr-roarrrr!

"What's that sound?" Henry whispered.

Wally gulped. Just a few more steps. Then he could dash into the storage room, grab a steak, and run away as fast as he could.

Nothing to fear, he told himself. He crept down another step. *Nothing to fear.* Something groaned nearby. *Nothing to fear . . .*

Wally set his paw on the last step.

Arrrrrrr!

A furry brown creature leaped out of the shadows and pounced at Wally and Henry. They toppled to the ground in a heap of fur and claws. Wally yowled. Henry screamed.

Then Wally heard a familiar laugh.

"Puggly?" Wally said nervously.

The little pup climbed off him. Wally squinted in the dark. The creature wasn't a monster-sized bilge rat. It was a pug-sized puppy playing another prank.

Puggly laughed and sneezed and cheered. "Got you again! That was pug-glorious! Piggly and I were working together to do a one-two prank punch. You jumped so high I thought your fur might fly off! What a scaredy-pup."

Wally was angry. "Just because I fell for your pranks, that doesn't prove I'm a chicken."

"I never said you were a chicken," Puggly barked. "Maybe a *kitten* . . ."

Before Wally could argue, the ship lurched to the side. They all went flying and smacked against the wall of the storage room. The boat rocked the other way, and they rolled again.

The raging sea was tossing the ship around like a bouncy ball. Up on deck, pups began to howl. A warning bell clanged. Captain Red Beard's booming voice rang out to every corner of the ship. "All paws on deck!"

A Dark and Stormy Day

Puggly, Wally, and Henry rushed up the stairs. On the main deck, the crewmates were scampering in all directions. All the puppy pirates were trying to get the ship ready to sail through the storm.

Some pups were tying down crates of food and supplies so they wouldn't wash overboard. Others were helping Captain Red Beard chart the best course through the rocking sea. The strongest pups were lowering the ship's sails.

The afternoon sky had gone from dark purplish-blue to black. It felt like night had come, even though they hadn't yet had dinner.

BOOOOOM.

BOOOOOM.

Wally felt each crack of thunder deep in his bones. Whenever lightning flashed, it was as though the whole world lit up for a few moments. Then everything went black again.

This was Wally's first storm at sea. He was trying very hard not to be afraid.

It seemed like everyone else had a job, but Wally didn't know what to do. He felt lost and a little dizzy from all the rolling waves. Still, he wanted to help.

As soon as he was sure he had his storm sea legs, Wally and Henry helped the pups who were bailing water. The giant waves washed onto

the ship. Wally and the others dumped buckets of it back overboard. The faster the waves came, the faster Wally and the others worked. But they couldn't work fast enough. Soon water was everywhere!

As the ship bounced over waves, the crew was tossed back and forth across the deck. Anything that wasn't tied down slipped and slid with the pups. In a bright flash of lightning, Wally spotted the ship's first mate, Curly, getting knocked to and fro. Curly was tiny, a bitty pouf of white poodle.

Lightning lit up the sky again. A huge wave tipped the ship far to one side. Curly nearly went overboard.

"Curly!" Wally shouted. He raced toward the first mate.

Curly was tough, but Wally knew even the toughest pups were no match for a big storm.

The ocean was huge and wild and scary. Curly was just a few pounds of muscle and brains. She kept clawing at the wooden deck, trying to keep her balance. But waves were pulling her toward the edge. Curly grabbed a rope in her teeth and held fast.

"Hold on!" Wally told Curly.

Curly growled something. Wally couldn't understand her with her mouth full of rope, but he knew what she was thinking. Curly was the smartest and fiercest pup on the ship. She wouldn't want to waste time saving her own tail when the crew needed her.

Wally had an idea. Together, Wally and Henry tied the smallest puppy pirates— Curly, Steak-Eye, and the pugs—to some of the largest pups using pieces of rope. If they were leashed together, Wally hoped, the pairs of pups wouldn't wash overboard when a big wave hit.

"I like your thinking, little Walty," Captain Red Beard said as Henry roped Curly to the captain.

Old Salt leaned against a deck rail for support. "In all my years at sea," he shouted over the wind, "I have never seen a storm like this!"

"We better get the knife jackets!" Red Beard shouted. Another wave pounded the ship.

Curly barked, "Say that again, sir?"

"The knife jackets!" Red Beard growled. "We should get out those cutie-patootie little orange vests that help things float in the water. We need to secure our swords and knives and cutlasses!"

Curly gave the captain a strange look. "Do you mean *life jackets,* sir?"

Captain Red Beard scratched his bearded chin. He shook the water from his ears. "Ah, yes. That makes more sense."

"Life jackets are for pups, not swords," Curly reminded him.

"Aye. I knew that," Red Beard barked. The waves were coming faster and higher. Every minute, the storm grew stronger and the wind blew harder. The next time lightning flashed, Wally saw a wave as tall as a mountain rolling toward the ship.

The captain spotted the wave at the same time. He raised his snout to the sky and howled. "Grab your life jackets, everyone! We're in for a wild ride."

Land Ho!

The wave looked like the giant mouth of a sea monster coming at them. "Stick together!" Curly barked.

"Hold on!" the captain ordered.

All the pups held on to each other. They made a huge chain of pups to be even more safe when a wave hit. As soon as the first giant wave had passed, another and another and another rolled in. But working together, the puppy pirates kept themselves afloat.

It was a cold, wet, windy afternoon. By the time the worst of the storm had passed, all the pups were hungry and tired. After what felt like hours, the sky began to brighten and the waves calmed. The captain ordered his crew to spread out across the *Salty Bone* to check for damage.

Steak-Eye rushed down to the galley to check on the food supplies and start dinner. Piggly and Puggly trotted along after him to help (and to get a snack).

Wally and Henry and a few other pups headed down to the sleeping quarters to gather up the wet beds and blankets. They hung everything on the deck rails to dry in the wind.

The largest pups worked on getting the sails back up. Meanwhile, Captain Red Beard and Curly studied their maps. The storm had blown the ship far off course. No one knew exactly where they were.

A fluffy Pomeranian named Marshmallow took the first shift in the crow's nest. He hoped the strong winds up in the watchtower would help dry his thick fur faster. He stretched his head up to let the wind blow his fluffy neck hair all around. That's when he spotted something. "Land ho!" Marshmallow barked.

Curly pulled out her spyglass and gazed at a dark lump on the horizon. "There's a large island straight ahead," she yipped.

"Let's head for it," ordered Captain Red Beard. "We'll drop anchor there for the night. It will help shelter our ship until we can be sure the storms have passed."

As they drew close to the island, the whole crew gathered on deck for a better view. Wally and Henry stood side by side. Wally put his front paws up on the rail and gazed out.

"In case you were wondering," Henry said,

pointing, "I'm pretty sure what we've got up ahead of us is a sea cove. If we sail the ship through that opening, we'll be in a protected bay. It's the best place for a ship like ours to wait out a storm."

They sailed closer and closer. As they neared the island, Wally could see that Henry was right. There was a small passage on one side of the island. It created a sort of channel that they could sail through.

The island was shaped like a horseshoe, with a protected pond in the center. Captain Red Beard steered the ship through the mouth of the cove, passing over a coral reef filled with colorful fish. Dolphins surrounded their boat, jumping and leaping on both sides of the ship as the puppy pirates sailed through the narrow pass.

Birdcalls echoed around them. The water was the color of an emerald and crystal clear. Wally had never seen a more beautiful place in all his life. It was like paradise.

But just as he began to think about a nice, long nap on deck under the warm sun, the sky darkened again. A huge black cloud blotted out the sun. Thunder cracked. Fat raindrops exploded on the deck.

"Captain!" Curly called out. She pointed toward the far side of the cove. "Look over yonder—the mouth of a cave. Let's head in there for shelter from the rain."

The boat sailed through the green-blue waters and straight toward a high rocky wall. In the middle of the rock face, a cave stretched open like a mouth. It was just wide and tall enough for their ship to fit through. Leaving paradise behind, the *Salty Bone* nosed into the

cave. The inside of the cave was almost black. Wally blinked fast, waiting for his eyes to adjust to the darkness.

Then he blinked again. Because it seemed his eyes were playing tricks on him. "Is that . . . ?" Wally peered into the darkness.

"Another ship," Henry gasped.

It was! A grand old ship was floating before them. Its sail was torn and faded, but Wally could make out the symbol painted on it: two

crossed bones. That was the sign of a *pirate ship*!

All the puppy pirates began chattering at once. "Silence!" Captain Red Beard ordered. He called out to the other ship, "Ahoy, there!"

His voice echoed on the cave walls. *Ahoy there . . . ahoy there . . . ahooooy there . . .*

The captain tried again. "Echo . . . *echo . . . echo . . . echo!*"

There was no answer. The other ship was old and run-down. It looked empty and a little spooky.

Puggly broke the silence just as a crack of thunder echoed outside the cave. "Could it be . . . Growlin' Grace's ghost ship?"

The puppy pirates began yipping and barking. *Could it be?*

"Let's board it and see!" Captain Red Beard said excitedly. "That will show Growlin' Grace just how brave we are!"

Spike whimpered and climbed into a storage crate. "What if the ghost of Growlin' Grace gets us?" he whined.

Old Salt coughed for attention. "Enough talk of ghosts," he said. "There's no such thing. If you ask me, I say we all get some sleep and check it out in the mornin' when we have more light. It's been a big day. Every last one of us needs a big meal and a good night's sleep."

Red Beard yawned. "You're right, Old Salt," he agreed. "That empty ship's not goin' anywhere tonight. We can explore it in the morning. For now, I want all pups to fill their bellies, and then it's straight to bed. Captain's orders!"

As the rest of the crew filed down the stairs to the dining hall, Wally couldn't stop staring at the strange old ship. He also couldn't stop thinking about how Piggly and Puggly had called him a scaredy-dog after falling for their pranks that afternoon. Wally knew he was brave! If he were the first puppy pirate to board that ship and find out if it *was* Growlin' Grace's ghost ship, wouldn't that prove to everyone just how brave he really was?

Before he could chicken out, Wally grabbed Henry's sleeve and tugged. They could eat and sleep later. Now it was time for an adventure!

Snooping Around

Wally waited until he and Henry were alone on deck. Then, very quietly, the two friends climbed into one of the ship's dinghies. Henry lowered the dinghy down to sea level. Then he rowed them through the water toward the strange ship. "Are you ready to explore this creepy old ship, mate?" Henry asked in a hushed whisper.

Wally said nothing. He pressed his head against his friend's knee. Henry could usually tell what Wally was thinking without him having to say a word. That's what made them best friends. He wondered if Henry knew he was a little nervous.

Probably.

After all, they were going against the captain's orders and sneaking onto a ship. And the ship was probably *haunted*. This was definitely the scariest thing they had ever done.

The water in the cave was still and black. Wally wondered what kind of creatures were swimming below them. Were they big, slimy beasts like the Sea Slug? Small, fast creatures with large teeth? He tried to put those thoughts out of his mind and focus on the adventure ahead.

Crack!

Their dinghy thudded against the hull of the other ship. Wally and Henry flinched at the noise. What if someone on the *Salty Bone* had heard?

They waited quietly for the sound of barks. But there was only silence.

"The coast is clear," Henry whispered a few minutes later. "Let's do this, mate!"

Henry climbed up to the old ship's main deck. Then he reached down and helped pull Wally aboard.

It was hard to see much with no light on board. Across the dark water, Wally could see the *Salty Bone,* all lit up. The main deck was empty, but the portholes belowdecks glowed with warm yellow light. Wally could picture his crewmates. They would be eating and singing now, then cuddling in their beds. He took a deep breath and tried not to worry himself. *Dark isn't scary,* he thought. *Ghosts aren't real.*

"Check it out," Henry said from the other side of the deck. "An old torch!" He held up something that looked like a stick. In the blackness, Wally heard a *pop,* then saw a blaze of light. "Now we can see where we're going. So let's go explore!"

Wally barked softly. "Yeah, let's go!"

Together, they crept across the deck and down the stairs of the old ship. They peeked into rooms as they walked along. There were portholes hiding behind lush velvet curtains. Old portraits of dogs in fussy hats and capes. Many bedrooms piled with dusty blankets and pillows. One room was empty except for a creaky old piano and hundreds of beautiful golden dog dishes.

"Whoa," Henry said, whistling softly. "Look at this."

Wally joined his friend in the next room. It was an old dining room of some kind. The tables were all set. Most of the dishes were dirty. "Yuck," Wally said, trying to breathe through his mouth. "It stinks in here."

"Do you see this?" Henry asked, pointing to a picture on the wall. "It says this is Growlin' Grace."

Wally stared up at the old painting. There she was: Growlin' Grace, the greatest puppy pirate who had ever lived. She was a sleek silver-gray pup with large eyes and a powerful body.

There were golden plates mounted on the dining room walls. Each one had the initials GG carved into it. "Think this was her boat?" Henry asked.

Wally felt a chill rush over his body. "It is," he said. "This must be Growlin' Grace's ghost ship." He put his nose down and sniffed at the corners of the room. He found a box of stale dog biscuits and another box filled with old, dried-up sausage treats. Wally was starving. He popped a biscuit into his mouth, chewing and crunching noisily.

"You know what we should do?" Henry asked with a smile. "Let's pretend this is *our* ship. Whaddya say?"

Wally wagged his tail. He loved to play pretend. Maybe if they had some fun on Growlin' Grace's ghost ship, he could stop worrying about what scary things were hiding in the corners.

"Ahoy, Captain Henry," Wally barked in his

deepest, toughest voice. He poked his head into
an old feathered hat and ran toward his friend.
"Yo ho harooo!"

Henry pulled a sword off the wall and waved
it through the air. "We are here for our swash-
buckling rescue! En garde!" He laughed.

Wally and Henry raced through room after room. They tried on musty clothes and

bounced on all the beds. For this one night, it was like they had their very own ship. Both of them loved getting to do whatever they wanted. They were in charge, with no one to answer to but themselves.

After they had explored and played for a long time, Henry and Wally returned to the dining room. Henry pushed some of the dirty dishes aside. Then he spread a blanket out on the table. He put a few biscuits and dried sausages in a pile in front of Wally. "Sir," Henry said, bowing low and laughing, "your dinner . . . is served."

Wally dug in. He filled himself with the sausage treats and biscuits, pretending it was a fancy feast. Henry chewed on a few sausages, too. Wally couldn't believe he had ever been afraid of being alone on Growlin' Grace's ship. He was having the best night ever! He loved playing on the big old ship, just him and Henry and their silly imaginations.

Suddenly, the torch sizzled and went out. "Uh-oh," Henry said quietly in the dark.

Outside, the storm had started up again. Even though they were anchored inside the cave, thunder echoed through the big wooden ship. Wally's heart beat faster. He swallowed his last biscuit. He listened for the sound of Henry's breathing. And that's when he heard it. . . .

Thump. Thump. Thump.

Maybe they weren't alone after all.

Creaks and Moans

Henry and Wally huddled together.

Wally hoped the noises he was hearing were just regular storm noises. Thunder, lightning, howling wind … Storms made all kinds of sounds. Right?

Ooooo-oooh!

It sounded like something howling. Wally gulped. He thought about how all the pups howled at thunder together on the *Salty Bone*.

That helped them be less afraid. He howled now in the dark. It felt very lonely to be howling all by himself. He longed for the rest of his crew.

"In case you were wondering, there's nothing to be afraid of," Henry said. But he didn't sound so sure. "Those noises are part of the storm, mate."

Wally hoped Henry was right.

All those strange sounds were very scary! Deep down, Wally knew there was no reason to be afraid of the dark. He and Henry just had to find their way above deck, climb into their dinghy, and sail back to their own ship. They could cuddle up under the covers, then come back to explore Growlin' Grace's ghost ship with everyone else in the morning.

It would be hard to find their way out of the creaky old ship without a light, but it wouldn't be impossible. Nothing was impossible for a puppy pirate. Besides, Wally had a nose that was great at searching.

Creak . . . creak . . .

Very near, something squeaked and whined.

That couldn't be the storm. Storms didn't creak or whine. And storms certainly didn't—

CRASH!

Wally and Henry both stood totally still. There was definitely something else on board Growlin' Grace's ship.

A ghost? Wally wondered. *Could Puggly's story be true?*

Then Wally had a crazy idea: what if Piggly and Puggly had seen Henry and Wally leaving the *Salty Bone* and followed? They could have snuck off the ship right after them. Then they might have sailed over to Growlin' Grace's ship in a dinghy of their own.

Maybe the pugs were just trying to play pranks again. Wally wasn't going to let the pugs scare him for the *third* time in one day. He knew what he had to do: he and Henry had to check things out!

Arrrrr-oooo!

A spooky howl rang through the empty halls of Growlin' Grace's ship. Wally tugged at Henry's sleeve, urging his friend to follow.

It was time for a ghost hunt.

Ghost Hunt

The darkness was heavy. It felt like they were walking through thick black mud. Wally couldn't even see his own nose. He led the way, sniffing and poking his paw out in front of him before each timid step.

They crept toward the stairs. As they climbed up to the main deck, Wally realized he could see a little more with each step up. Either it was getting brighter inside the cave . . .

or there was a light shining somewhere else on Growlin' Grace's ship.

"Avast," Henry said quietly when they got to the top of the stairs. "I think I hear something!" He peered around a corner. Wally did the same. He heard something rustling in the shadows near a stack of crates. Suddenly, a light flickered on the other side of the main deck.

"Over yonder," Wally said in a low voice. He put his head down and crept quietly across the deck. The hairs on the back of his neck stood up. His ears went flat. A quiet growl built in his throat. The light flashed again, and Wally stopped.

Crept forward.

Stopped again.

Something moved. Wally wanted to run— but he didn't. What if it *was* just the pugs? They weren't going to fool him again!

Wally put his nose to the ground and sniffed. He couldn't get a trace of Piggly *or* Puggly anywhere. He smelled something, though. A whiff of some creature he had never smelled before. He took another careful step forward. He tripped on a strange wire that was stretched across the center of the deck. A light flashed again.

Grrrrr-ahhh!

A white figure popped out of the shadows and flew straight at them.

"Ghost!" Henry screamed.

Wally didn't stop to think. He leaped at the ghost, trying to protect his best friend. Wally growled and yipped, grabbing for the ghost with his teeth. Henry stumbled backward and crashed into a pile of crates. The crates toppled and knocked Wally onto his side. By the time he stood up and shook himself off, the ghost was gone.

"That was pretty brave, mate!" Henry said, ruffling Wally's fur. "Whatever that was, I think you scared it away."

"Me? Brave?" Wally straightened up. He hadn't even thought about being brave. All he'd wanted to do was protect Henry. And he had! "I guess it *was* pretty brave," Wally said, wagging his tail. "Do you think I scared the ghost right off the ship?"

Henry didn't answer.

"Henry?" Wally barked, louder.

Henry brought his finger to his lips. "Shhh." Then, slowly, he pointed up at the crow's nest.

Something was moving up there in the dark.

Something white and glowing—and it was swooping straight for them!

Another flying ghost? Henry and Wally ducked. The ghost whooshed over their heads and off the side rail of the ship into the blackness.

"We've got to get out of here before it comes

back!" Wally yelped. This ship was definitely haunted.

Up on the bridge, another light flashed on, then off. From down below, Wally could see the big wheel that steered the ship beginning to turn all on its own. The curtains inside the steering cabin rustled. "What's in there?" Henry asked, shivering.

"I don't think I want to know," Wally said. Something moved behind them again. Wally spun around. "En garde!" he barked, trying to sound much braver than he felt.

There was no one there.

"We have to get back to the *Salty Bone*," Henry said. "Now." He sounded scared. Which made Wally even *more* scared. Henry was right. They needed to get off this haunted ship and back to their friends.

They tiptoed across the deck, back toward

their dinghy. They were almost there when Wally stopped in his tracks. His nose twitched.

"What is it, mate?" Henry whispered. "You smell a ghost?"

Wally shook his head. What he smelled was *fish*. And not rotten, moldy fish from hundreds of years ago. This was yummy, tasty, juicy fish. *Fresh* fish! Wally's stomach grumbled. He put his nose to the ground and followed the smell.

Ah-ha! There it was: a dog dish filled with tasty fish morsels. Wally licked the bowl gently. Could this be some kind of ghostly trap?

Nope. Nothing happened.

So he took a big piece of fish in his mouth and chewed. Then he wondered: *do ghosts eat fish?*

Treasure Trap

"I think there's something fishy about this ghost," Henry said.

"There's definitely something fishy about this fish," Wally said, his mouth full. He gulped down the rest of it. The bowl of fresh fish morsels made a perfect puppy dinner. Which made Wally curious: *what if the thing haunting the ship wasn't a ghost after all?*

What if it was another puppy?

Henry dug under a pile of maps and found an old lantern. He lit it, and a circle of light blazed around them. Now that they had light again, the ship felt a little less scary. The sound of the storm felt farther away somehow, too.

"This will light our way back to the *Salty Bone*," Henry said. "*If* we still want to go back?"

Wally wasn't so sure anymore. "I think there's another pup on this ship trying to scare us," Wally told him. If the whole point of this adventure was to prove they were brave, they couldn't run away now.

"I think we should find out what's making all these noises," Henry said. "What do you think, mate?"

Wally wagged his tail, and they set off into the darkness. They made their way up to the steering cabin. Wally poked his nose under the ship's wheel. Henry pulled back the curtains.

No puppies. No ghosts. The room seemed empty . . . except for one thing: a treasure chest!

"Avast!" Henry said, holding the lantern up to the large wooden chest. "This is even better than a ghost. You think there's treasure inside?"

There was only one way to find out.

Henry poked at the rusty lock. It fell apart at his touch.

"Let's open it!" Wally barked.

Henry pulled the lock off. "Yo ho ho," he said, grinning. "Pirate booty, here we come!" He put his hands on either side of the chest and lifted up. Henry grunted. The lid of the chest wouldn't budge. "It's stuck," he said, still grunting. The boy gave the chest a big kick, then tried again.

Pop! The lid of the chest popped open a few inches, then slammed closed again.

Henry lifted it up again. But no matter how hard Henry pushed, the chest wouldn't stay

open. Again and again he tried. But each time, he could only get it open a few inches and then it snapped closed.

"Hee hee hee hee hee!" Creepy laughter rang out around them. Wally's ears pricked up as the laughter echoed.

"Who's there?" Henry called into the darkness. He swung the lantern, trying to see out to the main deck.

A squeaky, high-pitched voice asked, "Trying to steal me treasure, are ya?"

"Show yourself!" Wally yapped. Could there be a ghost pirate after all?

"Hee hee hee hee hee hee hee!" The voice laughed and laughed, then began to cough.

Henry and Wally exchanged a look. What kind of ghost *coughs*?

"This is *our* ship," the scratchy voice whispered. The voice sounded like it was coming from somewhere nearby. Wally sniffed all around, trying to find the source of the laughter. Again, the voice squeaked, "You are trespassing, ya scurvy dog."

Wally whipped his head around. *There!* He was pretty sure the voice was coming from a huge pipe. "Say that again," he ordered. He wanted to make sure he was right before he set off to hunt it down.

"I *said*, you are trespassing, ya scurvy dog," the creature sighed.

Yep, Wally thought. *The spooky voice is coming through this pipe.* But where did the pipe lead? Somewhere outside the steering cabin, it seemed.

"No dog sneaks onto this ship without asking for trouble," the voice growled. "Dogs who trespass on this ship get punished."

"What about humans?" Wally barked. "You didn't say anything about humans!"

"Graggle!" the voice yipped. "Stinkbug! Plink!"

"Excuse me?" Wally said, speaking directly into the pipe.

"Don't try to trick me," squeaked the voice. "You know I meant humans, too. I'm not falling for your silly riddles. No one is allowed to sneak onto our ship. And I saw you two stinkers trying to steal our treasure."

"We didn't know it was your treasure!" Wally said. "We didn't know it belonged to anyone."

"A likely story," the voice squealed. "You were tryin' to steal it, all right, and anyone who tries to steal the treasure—" The door of the steering cabin flew open. Wally and Henry both froze. Something white rushed toward them. It was making horrible sounds—cries and moans and *yip-yip-yipp*ing!

Wally pounced. He got a mouthful of fabric. The white creature zoomed around the room as Wally tugged and tugged.

"Ah-ha!" Henry gasped. The white fabric came off and revealed a strange furry beast. "You're no ghost!"

A tiny, matted dog stood before them. "Oh, yeah? Says who?"

Henry shoved his lantern in front of the pup's face. "You're just a tiny dog!"

"Growlin' Grace was huge," Wally said. "You *can't* be her ghost."

The pup showed its teeth and growled. "So maybe I'm not Growlin' Grace's ghost. . . ."

That's when another creature burst into the steering cabin. In a huge, booming voice, it barked, "But *I* am!"

We Are the Weirdos

"You are *not* Growlin' Grace," Wally barked. The second dog was huge. But she was shaggy and brown and had very long, very dirty hair. Her tail swooshed like a piece of leafy seaweed. She looked nothing like the picture of Growlin' Grace he and Henry had seen on the dining room wall. "Who are you *really?*"

The smaller pup sighed and glared at the large dog. "I told you this wouldn't work."

The bigger pup grunted. "And I told *you* to stop coughing. Your cold ruined everything. What kind of ghost *coughs*?" She looked at Wally. "I'm right, right? It was the coughing that gave us away?"

"Who *are* you?" Henry said. He looked ready to fight. "Get back! We're not afraid of you!"

Wally stepped between Henry and the two strange pups. He could sense that these dogs weren't dangerous, but you could never be sure just from looking. "My name is Wally. I'm a puppy pirate. This is my best mate, Henry. We're both sailors on the *Salty Bone,*" he said. "You aren't really ghost pirates, are you?"

"Do we *look* like ghost pirates?" said the smaller dog. He closed one eye and squinted at Wally out of the other.

Wally looked them over. Then he stepped forward to sniff each one. Both pups were wearing very old-fashioned outfits—long, torn capes; lacy collars that smelled like dust; big, fancy hats. Wally was sure Puggly would be very jealous of the strange pups' fun clothes!

Wally decided they didn't look or smell like ghosts, though. They smelled like regular pups. He shook his head. "No, I don't think you are ghost pirates."

"Aye," said the larger dog. "We be the Weirdos."

"Huh?" Wally asked, cocking his head. "What are the Weirdos?"

"You mean you've never heard of us?" the tiny dog yapped.

"I'm sorry," Wally said. "But no, I haven't."

"I'm Millie," the big dog said. "And this little coughin' hair ball is Stink. Together, we are the Weirdos." Suddenly, Stink and Millie began to dance. In awful, tuneless voices they sang:

"We are the Weirdos!
We like to dance.
We are the Weirdos!
We wear cute pants!"

At the end of their song, Stink and Millie wiggled their paws and bowed their heads low. "Ta-da!" said Stink.

Henry giggled. Wally nudged his friend to be quiet. He could tell Stink and Millie were very proud of their song and dance. He said, "That was a very nice song."

"You hated it," grumped Stink.

"It's awful," growled Millie.

"No, no!" Wally insisted. "It's very nice. It's just . . . well, you don't actually *wear* pants. So I'm not sure it makes sense."

Stink and Millie glanced back at their hindquarters. Then they looked up at each other. "By golly, that dog is right," Stink said. "No *wonder* our song hasn't been working,

Millie. Ooh, ooh! What about this?" He sang:

> "We are the Weirdos!
> We like to dance!
> We are the Weirdos!
> We wear cute socks."

Stink grinned at Wally and said, "Eh? Is that better?"

"It doesn't rhyme!" argued Millie. "*Dance* and *socks* just don't sound right together."

"Have you thought about singing it this way?" asked Wally. He began to sing and dance, just like Stink and Millie. But he changed around a few words:

> "We are the Weirdos!
> We like to dance.
> We are the Weirdos!
> We don't wear pants!"

"That's it!" gasped Millie. "Aw, Wally. We've been working on that theme song for years and now it's fixed!"

Wally smiled. "Well, I'm glad I could help."

"You really haven't heard of us?" Millie asked. She hung her big head sadly. "But Stink said we be famous."

Wally shook his head. Henry, who had been working on trying to open the treasure chest, looked up. He said, "How do you open this thing, anyway?"

Stink gave him the stink eye. "Lift the latch." He trotted over and flipped open a latch on the side of the trunk. The lid flew open.

"Aw, shucks," Henry said, staring sadly into a trunk full of old clothes. "There's nothin' good in here."

"Nothin' good?" Stink shook his little head. "That there is a chest full o' fun!"

"Is that why you're here?" asked Millie. "To steal our fun? Are you thieves?"

"No, our ship got blown off course during a thunderstorm," Wally told them. "We sailed into this cave to seek shelter. That's when we found your ship. Henry and I just wanted to explore a little bit. We were wondering if maybe this was Growlin' Grace's ghost ship."

"Ah," said Stink. "Well, I suppose I can see why you might think that."

"*Is* it Growlin' Grace's missing ship?" Wally gasped. "Where is the rest of the crew?"

Stink sighed. Millie explained, "It's just the two of us now. And no, sirree, this is not Growlin' Grace's missing ship. Her ship was lost long ago."

Stink curled up in a tiny little ball while Millie told the Weirdos' tale. "Many, many years ago, Growlin' Grace ruled every drop of water in all the seas in all the world. She was the greatest pirate that ever lived. But one night, her ship sailed out of a battle and disappeared. No one knows exactly what happened, but Growlin' Grace was never heard from again."

"Was it a battle with the Sea Slug?" Wally

asked. "And is it true that her crew was afraid, so Growlin' Grace kicked them off the ship?"

"How dare you say somethin' so awful about such a great pirate captain!" Stink snapped. "Growlin' Grace was loyal to her crew until the very end."

"How do you know?" asked Wally.

"Because our great-great-great-grandmother sailed on that ship," said Millie, stomping her big, furry foot. "Our gran was the only pup anyone ever heard from again after Growlin' Grace's greatest battle. She got separated from the rest of the crew during the battle and ended up on this here ship."

"For many years, our family sailed around the world, searching for Grace and the ol' crew," Stink said sadly. "But the ship can't sail anymore, so now we have to wait for Growlin' Grace's ship to find us."

"You've been waiting here all alone?" Wally asked. He thought it sounded like a very lonely life.

"Not just waiting," Millie said. "Preparing. We practice being brave!"

"How?" Wally asked.

"We figure out ways to scare each other," Stink said. "Costumes. Booby traps. It's not often we get a chance to scare another pup. How did we do?"

Wally glanced at Henry, then said, "It's hard to scare us. We're pretty brave." Then he asked, "Aren't *you* ever scared? Being on this big ship, all by yourselves?"

"*Us?* Scared?" Millie repeated. She sounded furious. "Stink, kind sir, did this pup just call us scaredy-dogs?"

"I believe he did, good lady," Stink said, glaring.

Millie growled at Wally and Henry. "*Rarrr! Arrr-rarrr-rarrr!*" She put up her paws and wiggled them around in the air.

Wally thought it looked more silly than scary. Until Stink growled, "No one calls *us* lily-livered. Them's fighting words! En garde!"

Wanna Be a Weirdo?

"No, no!" Wally said quickly. He didn't want to fight with the Weirdos. "I didn't mean that you were cowards. I just thought it might get lonely out here, all alone."

"Oh," Stink said, scowling. "Well, why didn't you say so? We almost had to battle you!"

Millie hung her head. "I didn't wanna fight you, anyway," she muttered. "Not after you fixed our theme song." She gently licked her long, matted hair.

"Pirate life is more fun with a crew," Henry said suddenly. "In case you were wondering."

"We don't need anyone but each other," Millie said. "We've got no rules. No one to boss us around."

Stink added, "We get to do whatever we want, whenever we want. Well, until a ship like yours sails into our harbor. Then it's *showtime!*" The little pup began to get excited as he explained how their ship worked. "See, we set up a bunch of booby traps that make it look like our ship is haunted. That way, intruders will be spooked and stay far, far away."

"Have you had many intruders?" Wally asked. The sea cove was in the middle of the ocean. He had a hard time believing many ships just happened to sail by and stop for the night.

Millie grunted. "Just the one."

"Us?" Wally asked. "We're the first crew to have found you in here?"

"Maybe so," Stink said. "But we were ready for ya!"

"We didn't scare them at all," Millie told him in a low voice.

"Don't try to blame my cold again, lady," Stink said, then coughed.

"I suppose you're going to try to blame me for howling wrong?" Millie asked. "I told you, I howl how I howl!"

"Your *howls* were supposed to sound like ghost moans," Stink snapped. He turned to Wally. "Did she sound like a ghost to you?"

"Um," Wally said, looking from one Weirdo to the other.

"Were you a *little* bit scared?" Millie asked. She looked hopeful.

"A little," Wally admitted. "But we're pirates. We don't scare very easily."

"Well, I admire that about you, kid," Stink said. "Hey! Here's an idea: how about you two join our crew? Just think of all the fun we could have. The four of us could be Weirdos together!"

"Why do you call yourselves the Weirdos, anyway?" Wally asked.

"That's what Growlin' Grace used to call her crew," said Stink. "She liked that she had a pack full of odd dogs who thought a little differently. They all had strange personalities and even stranger ideas about pirating life. So she called herself and her crew the Weirdos. We liked it, so we kept it."

"So whaddya say?" Millie asked. "You want to come live with us and be a Weirdo? You can help us run the ghost ship. Be a part of our plays, spend your days singing and dancing?"

"What else do you do on board the ship?" Wally asked. He wondered what life was like for the Weirdos. Did they ever get bored, just the two of them?

"We tell stories," said Stink.

"Well, we just tell the *one* story," added Millie. "Stink likes when I tell my story about sea turtles. So I tell it over and over and over again. It's the only one I know."

On the *Salty Bone,* there were loads of tales to tell. Old Salt remembered so many fun adventures from all his years at sea. And the pugs were great at making up stories. Wally felt sad that the Weirdos had only the one story to share.

"What do you eat?" Wally asked. He thought of the stale biscuits and sausage treats he had found in the old dining room. Then he thought about Steak-Eye's stew and the special meals they got sometimes.

"Biscuits and such," Stink said. "You get used to it. But sometimes Millie catches fish in the harbor, and then we eat like kings for a few days. Admit it, life sounds grand here with us, doesn't it?"

Wally wasn't sure how to tell them that it did *not* sound grand. Life on board the Weirdos' ship sounded boring and lonely! Just two pups, doing the same thing day after day? He felt so lucky he got to be a part of the *Salty Bone* crew and go on new adventures all the time. "Um . . . ," Wally began.

Bam!

Something thumped into the side of the ship. There were loud barks and howls coming from the water below.

"Someone's here!" Stink and Millie leaped up.

Henry peered out the window, then turned and announced, "It's our crew, mate! The rest of

the crew from the *Salty Bone* are coming aboard the ghost ship."

"Yo ho ho," barked Stink. "A second chance to spook some pups!"

"Now you'll see how scary we can be." Millie howled as loud as she could. "*Arrrrr-ooooo!* Ghost pirates, action!"

The Search Crew

"Wait!" Wally begged. "Don't spook them yet." He had an idea. But first he had to stop the Weirdos from scaring away his crew.

The two Weirdos cocked their heads. Millie asked, "Why not?"

"Do you want to help?" Stink whispered. "We can get you a spooky costume and show you how to get the booby traps set up and everything!"

"We don't have time for that now," Millie

argued. "We have to put our spook plan in place! It's our big moment. Let's show them that this lord and lady are ready for *action*." Once again, she waggled her paws in the air. Wally tried to hold back his laughter.

"Yeah, because what if they've come to steal our treasure?" Stink said suspiciously. "They can't have it!"

"I thought you didn't have any treasure," Wally said.

"Well . . . that's a fair point. But if we did, we wouldn't let them have it," Stink said.

"Captain Red Beard would never try to steal your treasure," Wally insisted. "And I can prove it to you, if you give me a chance."

"How are you going to do that?" Millie woofed.

Henry peeked up over the edge of the ship's huge steering wheel. After a long night aboard the ghost ship, the sun had begun to rise. A thin shaft of light was slipping through the mouth of the cave. Everything was bathed in a soft, warm glow. "Should we spy on 'em for a little while?" Henry suggested.

The Weirdos thought about that for a minute. "Spying . . . I like the sound of that," Millie said. "Let's do it!"

Henry, Wally, and the Weirdos watched the puppy pirate crew from their hiding spot in the steering cabin. They watched Captain Red Beard, the pugs, Curly, and the rest of the gang board the ghost ship.

"Fan out!" Wally heard Red Beard call out. "Let's take a lookie-loo and see what we have here!"

"Sir?" Curly asked. "Should I gather up a team of pups and look for little Wally and his boy?"

"They're searching for us?" Wally gasped,

turning to Henry. He was surprised anyone had even noticed they were gone!

"They must miss you," Stink said in Wally's ear.

Millie bowed her huge head low. "I wish someone were searching for *us*."

Wally felt warm and happy when he realized the whole crew had come looking for them.

"Yes, Curly," Red Beard said from down below. "We *must* find little Walty. Our crew isn't complete without him and his human. If we lost them somewhere in the storm . . ." The captain shook his head sadly. "I don't know what I'd do."

"We'll find them," Curly said. "Whatever it takes. Maybe they just came over here in search of a little adventure."

"This ship sure does seem like a good place for an adventure," Captain Red Beard said, looking around. "You can see it was once a mighty nice vessel. But she could use a little love now." Red Beard pressed his paw against one of the deck rails. A piece of the rail fell away and crashed into the water with a loud *splash!*

"He's breaking our ship," Millie growled quietly. "And how dare he say she could use a little love—our ship is perfect!"

"That's not true," Stink pointed out. "She can't even sail anymore. She just sits here in this cave like a big, lazy walrus."

Wally shushed them.

Captain Red Beard called for the rest of the crew's attention. He said, "While Curly and the pugs search for Walty, I want the rest of you to put this ship back in order. If it really *is* Growlin' Grace's ghost ship . . . well, a mighty fine pirate like Grace deserves the nicest ship on the sea. Let's see what we can do to make her ship shine again!"

"They're going to fix our ship?" Stink whispered.

Soon it was clear that was *exactly* what Red Beard and the crew had in mind. Working together, the pups from the *Salty Bone* swabbed the decks and patched the sails and fixed up the broken rails.

"They're taking apart our ghostly booby traps," Millie moaned.

Stink nudged her and said, "But they're turning our ship back into the beauty she once was!"

Wally, Henry, and the Weirdos watched. While they worked, the other pups from the *Salty Bone* talked about all the great adventures Growlin' Grace must have had many moons ago. Millie sighed and covered her nose with her paws.

"What's wrong?" Wally asked her.

"I would like to have some adventures," she said. "They sound like fun."

Stink squeaked, "It's hard to be a brave and adventurous pirate when you're just sitting around on an empty ship in a cave all day and night."

"It looks like you were right to stop us from

scaring your crew away," Millie told Wally. "I'm glad I got to hear all those stories."

"And they fixed our ship!" Stink barked. "We should thank them."

"I think Captain Red Beard would really like to meet you," said Wally. "But first . . . want to help me do something fun?"

"You fixed our song, Wally," Millie woofed. "We owe you. What do you want us to do?"

Henry pointed at two little pugs scurrying across the deck. They looked like they were up to something, as usual. "Hey, mate, it looks like Piggly and Puggly are plotting another prank. What do you think?"

Wally grinned at Henry. This time, the pugs weren't the only ones with a plan. "I think we have some pug friends who could use a little visit from two ghost pirates!"

The Ghost Ship

Millie and Stink couldn't wait to put all their ghostly tricks to good use. And Wally couldn't wait to spook Piggly and Puggly right out of their wrinkled skin.

Wally put the Weirdos in charge of the plan. After all, they knew their ship best.

Stink muttered to himself for a minute, then launched into the treasure chest. He pawed and dug at the pile of old clothes. Hats flew this way and that. Capes were soon scattered all over the floor of the steering cabin. Once everything was out of the old treasure chest, Wally could see that there was a huge hole at the bottom of the trunk!

"Whoa," Henry said, gazing into the chest. "In case you were wondering? I'm pretty sure that's a secret passage or something!"

Millie and Stink both gave him a funny look. "Nice guess," Millie said. "We have secret passages like this set up all over the ship. This one here takes us down to the galley. If you crawl through that big pipe over there, it's a shortcut to our sleeping quarters."

Before they climbed into the secret passageway, all four of them had to put on costumes. There was even one that mostly fit Henry. When he was dressed, Wally looked down at himself and giggled. In his dusty white robe, he looked just like a ghost pirate! This was going to be the best pug prank in history.

The three pups wiggled into the secret passage. Henry crawled through behind them. He had to make himself very small to fit in the tight space.

Slowly, quietly, they crept along the passageway until they reached the end. It opened into a shadowy corner in the dining room. Wally caught his breath—Piggly and Puggly were snacking only a few feet away!

"I smell Wally," Piggly said, gobbling up stale biscuits as quickly as she could. "He's been in here—the pup's scent is everywhere."

"Aye," agreed Puggly. She nosed open a tin of fish and took a bite. "Maybe we should look around in here a little more? Make sure he's not hidin' somewhere?"

"Aye," Piggly grunted.

Wally tried not to laugh. He was hiding, all right—but he would pounce long before the pugs had a chance to find him!

Quiet as could be, Wally crept toward the pugs. Henry and the Weirdos followed behind him. They all ducked low and hid under a tablecloth. *"Piggly . . . ,"* Millie whispered.

"What's that?" Piggly said, dropping her biscuit. She spun around and around on her squat legs. Wally tried to keep himself from laughing.

"Pugglyyyyyyyyy . . . ," Stink squeaked.

"Eh?" Puggly said, hiding behind a chair. "Who's there?"

"Ooooo-ooooh," Henry moaned.

"Arrrr-ooooo!" Wally joined the chorus of moans and groans.

Piggly and Puggly exchanged a look. "Is that—" Piggly whined. She tried to hide her chubby body under a bench.

"Growlin' Grace's ghost!" Puggly shrieked. She leaped up on a table, scattering tins of fish everywhere. Platters flew up in the air. All the noise frightened the pugs even *more*.

Piggly and Puggly scrambled to hide. Then Wally and the others jumped out from their hiding place. When the pugs saw the four figures in ghostly costumes, they both yelped.

"Ghosts!" Piggly barked. "Run!" She and her

sister raced across the tabletops toward the door. Puggly slipped on a plate, and her feet flew out from under her. She tumbled to the floor with a loud *oof!*

"Gotcha!" Wally threw off his costume.

"Wally?" Piggly asked, creeping forward.

"'Tis me," Wally cheered. "I've been on board

this ghost ship all night! You told me I was a scaredy-pup, so Henry and I snuck over here to prove you wrong. Look who's a scaredy-pup now!"

Piggly laughed and laughed. She loved a good prank, even when the joke was on her. "You're right, Wally. You got us good."

Puggly shook her head. "But we were just teasing you before, Wally. You didn't need to prove how brave you are, kid! You've proven your courage a million times."

Wally beamed. He knew that was true, but it felt good to hear it from someone other than Henry.

Piggly grunted and gaped at the two Weirdos. "Ahoy. Who are you?"

"We be the Weirdos!" Millie woofed. She looked at Puggly's outfit and said, "I like your boots."

"And I like *your* capes," Puggly said. "Very fancy."

While the pugs and the Weirdos sniffed at each other, the rest of the crew came rushing into the dining room. "We heard the pugs' warning barks!" Captain Red Beard gasped. "What's the problem?"

"There is no problem, sir," said Wally. He stepped forward. "Just playing a little prank."

"Walty!" Red Beard woofed happily when he saw his cabin boy. "There you are!"

Wally nodded and said, "Captain, there are a couple of puppy pirates I want you to meet. This is Stink, and this is Millie. They call themselves the Weirdos."

To say hello, Stink and Millie launched into their song again. They spun and danced:

> **"We are the Weirdos!**
> **We like to dance!**

We are the Weirdos!
We don't wear pants!"

"Ta-da!" said Stink. Millie wiggled her paws and bowed. Wally laughed and cheered.

Red Beard's eyes opened wide. He stared at the two Weirdos. "Weirdos, you say?"

"Aye, aye, sir," said Stink.

"As in, Growlin' Grace's Weirdos?" Red Beard looked like he'd seen a ghost.

"Yes, sir." Millie nodded her big head. "Our great-great-great-gran was one of Growlin' Grace's own. We are the last in a long line of Weirdos—and proud of it!"

"Well, well," said Red Beard. "I never . . ."

"You've heard of us?" asked Stink.

Red Beard barked. "Heard of you? Of *course* I've heard of you! I've been wantin' to meet a Weirdo all my seafaring life!"

Welcome Aboard

"You really have heard of us?" Millie asked, her big eyes open wide. "This gent and myself? The last of the Weirdos?"

"Aye! The Weirdos are famous," Red Beard said. "Do you live on this here ship?"

"We do," said Stink. "Though it's not Growlin' Grace's ship, we have tried our best to make it look like hers. We used to sail all over the world, searching for Growlin' Grace."

"Where's the rest of your crew?" Curly asked them.

Millie and Stink glanced at each other. "You're lookin' at it," said Millie.

Wally pulled the captain and Curly aside. He whispered his big idea into their ears. Captain Red Beard broke into a huge smile. "I like the way you think, little Walty." He turned to the Weirdos and said, "How would you like to join our crew? We would love to have a few Weirdos on board."

Stink's tail began to wag, and he said, "Come sail with you?"

"Ooh! Ooh!" Millie woofed. "Here's a nifty idea. What if our ship sailed alongside yours, off into the wide blue ocean? We could be a fleet."

"Feet?" Red Beard asked. He glanced at Henry. "Like the human's stinky feet?"

"Fleet, sir," Stink explained. "We would be a

team of ships, sailing together."

"Ah, of course, a *fleet*. I just didn't hear you the first time. Hmm," said Captain Red Beard. "But your ship isn't sea-worthy, is she?"

"You fixed it!" Millie barked. "She looks good as new now. Time to sail away into the sunset, eh?"

Curly stepped forward and said, "Your ship has been cleaned up, aye. But I'm sorry to say, she still can't sail."

"So we would have to leave our ship?" Millie asked. "Leave it behind?"

"For now," Wally told them. "We could come back and check on it whenever we sail this way. Don't you think this is what Growlin' Grace would have wanted? To see the last of her Weirdos out on brave pirate adventures?"

Stink and Millie looked at each other. "Think of all the new stories we'd get to hear," Stink said quietly.

"And all the adventures we'd get to go on," Millie added. "Then we could tell our own stories."

"Sounds to me like we have two new members of our crew," Red Beard barked. "Welcome aboard, Weirdos!"

For the rest of the afternoon, the crew of the *Salty Bone* worked with Stink and Millie to pack up a few items on their ship. Captain Red Beard gathered up the golden bowls from the piano room. He explained that it would be risky to leave such beautiful treasures behind.

Curly suggested they take the portrait of Growlin' Grace to hang in Stink and Millie's new quarters. Puggly helped to pack up all the best costumes. Steak-Eye and Piggly worked together to clean the dining room. The rest of the crew tidied the other rooms on board. They all wanted to leave the ship nice and neat for the next time they visited.

When it was finally time to leave, Stink and Millie took one final lap around their ship. Their last stop was the piano room. Stink pranced across the keys, singing quietly under his breath. Millie joined him, humming the tune of "We Are the Weirdos" one last time. Then they hopped in a dinghy and boarded the *Salty Bone* with the rest of their new crew.

As the *Salty Bone* sailed out of the cave, Wally, Henry, and the pugs joined their new friends at the ship's rail. They watched as Stink and Millie's ship seemed to disappear inside the cave. Millie hung her huge head and said, "Goodbye, fine ship. Goodbye, theme song."

"Aw, quit lookin' so sad," Piggly said, her gold tooth glinting in the setting sun. "You don't have to stop singing just because you're leaving your ship."

"We don't?" Millie said.

"Nah," said Puggly. "In fact, your song's gonna sound even better here on the *Salty Bone*!

Every pirate shanty sounds mighty fine with more voices."

Suddenly, the rest of the crew came bounding out onto the main deck. They were all wearing costumes from the Weirdos' ship! And they were all dancing and singing:

"We are the Weirdos!
We like to dance!
We are the Weirdos!
We don't wear pants!
We all are Weirdos!
We're on our way!
We all are Weirdos!
You're here to stay!"

Millie and Stink joined in. Before long, everyone was laughing and singing together. When the song ended, the puppy pirates cheered. Then Wally barked, "We're *all* Weirdos now! Welcome aboard, mateys!"

Turn the page
to learn how
to draw a
Puppy Pirate!

How to Draw a Puppy Pirate!

Follow the steps below to draw a favorite Puppy Pirate—Wally!

Step 1: Draw a square shape for the body. Add a rectangle to the top for the head. Draw a series of slanted rectangles for the arms and legs.

Step 2: Add more rectangles for the ears, snout and nose, hands, overalls, and feet. To make the sword, draw one straight line connected with a curved line. Don't forget to add circles for the eyes!

Step 3: Now that you have the basic shapes in place, you can start adding curves on top of your basic drawing to make it look smoother. You can also put in more details, like fingers, a mouth, toes, and a tail.

Step 4: Continue adding details like wrinkles, eyebrows, and pockets. Now you have a finished drawing of Wally!

Hunting for Henry

Wally found a note from Henry, but it's in code. Can you tell what it says?

Piggly's Puzzle

Piggly needs your help! Puggly has written her a message, but it's in code. Use the key below to unlock the answer.

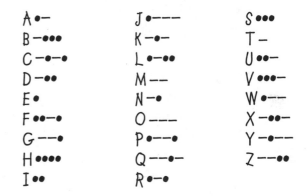

A •—   J •———   S •••
B —•••   K —•—   T —
C —•—•   L •—••   U ••—
D —••   M ——   V •••—
E •   N —•   W •——
F ••—•   O ———   X —••—
G ——•   P •——•   Y —•—•
H ••••   Q ——•—   Z ——••
I ••   R •—•

Puppy Pirates vs. Kitten Pirates

Grab your fellow pirate friends and
race to swab the decks!

You will need:
A large open floor space
5 Ping-Pong balls in one color
5 Ping-Pong balls in a different color
2 brooms

How to play:

1. Split your friends into two crews: one for Puppy Pirates, one for Kitten Pirates. Each team should select a captain. The captain will split their crew in half and send one half of the team to the opposite side of the room.

2. Each team gets a broom and five Ping-Pong balls in the same color. On the word "Go!" one pirate from each crew must sweep their balls to the other side of the room. Once they get there, the next crew member must sweep their team's Ping-Pong balls back to the other side.

3. Continue until every player has had a turn. The crew to finish first wins the game!

All paws on deck!

Another Puppy Pirates adventure
is on the horizon.
Here's a sneak peek at

Search for the Sea Monster

Wally could hear something breathing very loudly.

And the *something* sounded close.

Wally's best friend, a boy named Henry, was asleep in the next bunk. The *something* snorted and snuffled. It sounded like something *big*. But Henry only giggled in his sleep, then rolled over.

Wally would have to handle this himself.

But what *was* this? It sounded like a monster with a stuffed-up nose. Wally gasped. Could there be a monster hidden under his bed? Wally nosed around the floor. He was careful not to get too close to the dark space under the bed.

The raspy breathing got louder and louder. The fur on the back of Wally's neck stood tall. He decided to wake Henry after all.

Wally put his paws on Henry's bunk and licked his best friend's nose.

"Eh?" Henry muttered sleepily.

"Monster," Wally whispered. He pointed his paw toward the space below their bunks. "Under there."

Henry's eyes got very wide. "In case you were wondering?" he whispered. "I don't like that sound. It's creepy." He tugged his blanket over his head.

The creature's breathing echoed in the dark cabin.

In, out, in, out.

"What could it be?" Henry said very quietly.

There was only one way to find out.